LITTLE CRITTER'S
JOKE BOOK

BY MERCER MAYER

For Caroline Hall

A GOLDEN BOOK • NEW YORK

Western Publishing Company, Inc., Racine, Wisconsin 53404

Library of Congress Catalog Card Number: 93-77751   ISBN: 0-307-12790-7/ISBN: 0-307-62790-X (lib. bdg.)   A MCMXCIII

SCHOOL DAZE

Classmate: Were the test questions hard, Little Critter?

Little Critter: *The questions were easy.*
It was the answers I had trouble with.

Mom: How did you do
on your first day of school?

Little Critter: *Not very well, I guess.*
I have to go back tomorrow.

Teacher: Little Critter, you missed school yesterday, didn't you?

Little Critter: *Not at all.*

Teacher: Little Critter, I want you to spell *mouse*.
Little Critter: *M-O-U-S.*
Teacher: But what's on the end?
Little Critter: *A tail!*

ALL WET

Friend: Little Critter, how did you come to fall in the pond?

Little Critter: *I didn't come to fall in. I came to fish.*

How do you stop a skunk from smelling?

What kind of pets make the best music?

What do you get if you cross a centipede with a parrot?

AND I'LL GIVE YOU THE ANSWER

(See previous page for the riddles.)

Hold his nose.

Trum-pets.

A walkie-talkie.

THE NEW BABY

How do you make a baby buggy?

Tickle his toes.

JUST CRAZY CRITTERS

What do you call
a two-ton critter?

Sir!

Where does a two-ton critter sleep?

Anywhere he wants to!

What kinds of umbrellas do critters use in the rain?

Wet ones!

Why do critters make better friends than elephants?

Try cuddling an elephant and you'll find out.

What kind of bow is impossible to tie?

A rainbow.

What has a head like a cat, eyes like a cat, a tail like a cat, but isn't a cat?

A kitten.

What runs around a yard without moving?

A fence.

Why can't a bicycle stand by itself?

Because it's two-tired.

What do you call a cow that eats grass?

A lawn moower.

Little Critter: Does Ginger bite?

Friend: *No, Ginger snaps.*

MORE RIDDLES...
(Turn the page for the answers.)

What time is it when an elephant sits on a fence?

Why do birds fly south in the winter?

What is the hardest part about learning to ice-skate?

AND MORE ANSWERS
(See previous page for the riddles.)

Time to fix the fence.

Because it's too far to walk.

The ice.

JUST ASK A SILLY QUESTION

Teacher: Little Critter, what do you mean by crawling into the classroom at three minutes after nine?

Little Critter: *You said never to walk in late.*

JUST ME AND MY DAD

Dad: What happened to your bicycle?

Little Critter: *Coming home, I rode into the wrong driveway and hit a tree we don't have!*

Dad: Little Critter, it's time for your violin lesson.

Little Critter: *Oh, fiddle.*

Little Critter: I can't walk any farther. My shoes hurt.
Dad: That's because you have them on the wrong feet.
Little Critter: *But these are the only feet I have!*

Little Critter: What's worse than finding a worm in an apple?

Dad: *Finding half a worm!*

What gives milk and has one horn?

A milk truck.

Why did the rooster cross the road?

To show he wasn't chicken.

What runs and whistles but can't talk?

A train.

What's black and white and bounces?

A panda on a pogo stick.

What is gray, has four legs, big ears, a tail, and a trunk?

A mouse going on vacation.

How can you knock over a full glass
without spilling any water?

Knock over a full glass of milk instead.

JUST ME AND MY BABY-SITTER

Baby-Sitter: Little Critter, what did you learn in school today?
Little Critter: I learned *"Yes, Sir. No, Sir. Yes, Ma'am and No, Ma'am."*
Baby-Sitter: You did?
Little Critter: *Yep!*

KNOCK, KNOCKS

Knock, knock.
Who's there?
Soup.
Soup who?

Soup-er Critter!

Knock, knock.
Who's there?
Owl.
Owl who?
Owl you know unless
you open the door?

Knock, knock.
Who's there?
Max.
Max who?
Max no difference.
Just open the door!

Knock, knock.
Who's there?
Police.
Police who?
Police let me in.
It's cold out here!

KNOCK, KNOCK FOR THE LAST TIME

Knock, knock.
Who's there?
Tail.
Tail who?

Tail all your friends about this book!